First published in *The Adventures of Mr Toad* 1998
by Walker Books Ltd, 87 Vauxhall Walk, London SE11 5HJ

This edition produced 2004 for
The Book People Ltd, Hall Wood Avenue,
Haydock, St Helens WA11 9UL

2 4 6 8 10 9 7 5 3 1

Illustrations © 1998 Inga Moore

The right of Inga Moore to be identified as illustrator of this work has been asserted
by her in accordance with the Copyright, Designs and Patents Act 1988

This book has been typeset in Bembo

Printed in China

British Library Cataloguing in Publication Data:
a catalogue record for this book is available from the British Library

ISBN 1-84428-974-5

www.walkerbooks.co.uk

Mr Toad

from
The Wind in the Willows

Written by
KENNETH GRAHAME

Abridged and illustrated by
INGA MOORE

TED SMART

Mr Toad

It was a bright morning in the early part of summer; the river had resumed its wonted banks, and a hot sun seemed to be pulling everything green and bushy up out of the earth, as if by strings. The Mole and the Water Rat had been up since dawn, busy on matters connected with boats and the boating season; painting and varnishing, mending paddles, repairing cushions, hunting for missing boat-hooks, and so on; and were finishing breakfast in their little parlour and discussing their plans for the day, when a heavy knock sounded at the door.

"Bother!" said the Rat, all over egg. "See who it is, Mole, like a good chap, since you've finished."

The Mole went to attend the summons, and the Rat heard him utter a cry of surprise. Then he flung the parlour door open, and announced with much importance, "Mr Badger!"

This was a wonderful thing, indeed, that the Badger should call on them, or on anybody. He generally had to be caught, if you wanted him, as he slipped quietly along a hedgerow of an early morning or a late evening, or else hunted up in his own house in the middle of the wood.

The Badger strode into the room, and stood looking at the two animals with an expression full of seriousness.

"The hour has come!" he said.

"What hour?" asked the Rat uneasily, glancing at the clock.

"*Whose* hour, you should say," replied the Badger. "Why, Toad's hour! The hour to take Toad in hand!"

"Hooray!" cried the Mole delightedly. "*We'll* teach him to be a sensible Toad!"

"This very morning," continued the Badger, "another new and exceptionally powerful motor-car will arrive at Toad Hall on approval or return."

"We ought to do something," said the Rat gravely. "He had another smash-up only last week, and a bad one. That coach-house of his is piled to the roof with fragments of motor-cars, none of them bigger than your hat!"

"He's been in hospital three times," put in the Mole; "and as for the fines he's had to pay, it's simply awful to think of."

"Yes," continued the Rat, "Toad's rich, we all know; but he's not a millionaire. And he's a hopelessly bad driver, and quite regardless of law and order. Killed or ruined – it's got to be one of the two, sooner or later."

"We must be up and doing," said the Badger, "ere it is too late. You two will accompany me instantly to Toad Hall."

"Right you are!" cried the Rat, starting up. "We'll rescue the poor animal!"

"We'll take him seriously in hand," went on the Badger. "We'll stand no nonsense whatever. We'll bring him back to reason, by force if need be. We'll *make* him be a sensible Toad."

They set off up the road on their mission, and reached Toad Hall to find, as the Badger had anticipated, a shiny new motor-car, of great size, painted a bright red, standing in front of the house. As they neared the door it was flung open, and Mr Toad, arrayed in goggles, cap, gaiters, and enormous overcoat, came swaggering down the steps.

"Hullo! you fellows!" he cried. "You're just in time to come for a jolly – a jolly – for a – er jolly—"

The Badger strode up the steps. "Take him inside," he said to his companions. Then he turned to the chauffeur in charge of the new motor-car.

"I'm afraid you won't be wanted today," he said. "Mr Toad has changed his mind. He will not require the car."

"Now, then!" he said to the Toad, when the four of them stood in the hall, "first, take those ridiculous things off!"

"Shan't!" replied Toad, with spirit. "What is the meaning of this? I demand an explanation."

They had to lay Toad out on the floor, kicking and calling all sorts of names, before they could get his motor-clothes off him bit by bit, and they stood him up on his legs again. Now he was merely Toad, and no longer the Terror of the Highway, he giggled feebly.

"You knew it must come to this sooner or later, Toad," the Badger explained severely. "You've disregarded all the warnings we've given you, you're getting us animals a bad name in the district by your furious driving and your smashes and your rows with the police. But we never allow our friends to make fools of themselves beyond a certain limit; and that limit you've reached. You've often asked us to come and stay with you, Toad; well, now we're going to. When you are sorry for what you've done, and see the folly of it, and you promise never to touch a motor-car again, we may quit, but not before. Take him upstairs, you two, and lock him in his bedroom."

"It's for your own good, Toady," said the Rat kindly, as Toad, kicking and struggling, was hauled upstairs by his two friends. "Think what fun we shall all have together, just as we used to, when you've quite got over this – this painful attack of yours! No more of those incidents with the police," he said, as they thrust him into his bedroom.

"No more weeks in hospital, being ordered about by nurses," added the Mole, turning the key on him.

They descended the stair, Toad shouting abuse at them through the keyhole.

"It's going to be a tedious business," said the Badger, sighing. "I've never seen Toad so determined. However, we will see it out. He must never be left an instant unguarded. We shall take it in turns to be with him, till the poison is out of his system."

They arranged watches accordingly. Each animal took turns to sleep in Toad's room at night, and they divided the day between them. At first Toad was very trying to his guardians. He would arrange bedroom chairs in rude resemblance of a motor-car and crouch on them, bent forward, staring fixedly ahead, making uncouth, ghastly noises, till the climax was reached, when, turning a complete somersault, he would lie prostrate amidst the ruins of the chairs, completely satisfied for the moment. As time passed, however, these seizures grew less frequent, and his friends strove to divert his mind into fresh channels. But his interest in other matters did not seem to revive, and he grew apparently languid and depressed.

One fine morning the Rat, whose turn it was to go on duty, went upstairs to relieve Badger, whom he found fidgeting to be off and stretch his legs. "Toad's still in bed," he told the Rat, outside the door. "Can't get much out of him, except, 'O, leave him alone.' Now, you look out, Rat! When Toad's quiet, he's at his artfullest."

"How are you today, old chap?" inquired the Rat cheerfully, as he approached Toad's bedside.

A feeble voice replied, "Thank you, Ratty! So good of you to inquire! How are you yourself, and the excellent Mole?"

"O, *we're* all right," replied the Rat. "Mole is going out for a run with Badger. So you and I will spend a pleasant morning together. Now jump up, there's a good fellow!"

"Dear Rat," murmured Toad, "I am far from 'jumping up'. I beg you – step round to the village and fetch the doctor."

"What do you want a doctor for?" inquired the Rat, coming closer and examining him. He certainly lay very still and flat, and his voice was weaker and his manner changed.

"Surely you have noticed—" murmured Toad. "Tomorrow, indeed, you may be saying, 'O, if only I had noticed sooner! If only I had done something!' But never mind – forget I asked."

"Look here, old man," said the Rat, beginning to get rather alarmed, "of course I'll fetch a doctor, if you really want him."

"And – would you mind," said Toad, with a sad smile, "at the same time asking the lawyer to step up? There are moments – a moment – when one must face disagreeable tasks."

"A lawyer! He must be bad!" the Rat said to himself, as he hurried from the room, not forgetting to lock the door behind him. "I've known Toad fancy himself frightfully bad before; but I've never heard him ask for a lawyer! If there's nothing the matter, the doctor will tell him he's an old ass, and cheer him up. I'd better go; it won't take long." So he ran off to the village on his errand of mercy.

The Toad, who had hopped lightly out of bed as soon as he heard the key turned in the lock, watched him from the window till he disappeared down the carriage-drive. Then he dressed quickly in his smartest suit, filled his pockets with cash from a drawer, and next, knotting the sheets from his bed together and tying one end round the central mullion of the Tudor window which formed such a feature of his bedroom, he scrambled out, slid to the ground, and, taking the opposite direction to the Rat, marched off whistling a merry tune.

It was a gloomy luncheon for Rat when the Badger and the Mole returned. The Badger's remarks may be imagined; even the Mole could not help saying, "You've been a bit of a duffer this time, Ratty! Toad, too, of all animals!"

"He did it awfully well," said the crestfallen Rat.

"He did *you* awfully well!" rejoined the Badger hotly.

Meanwhile, Toad, gay and irresponsible, was walking along the high road, some miles from home. At first he had taken by-paths, and crossed many fields, and changed his course several times, in case of pursuit; but now, feeling safe from recapture, and the sun smiling brightly on him, and all nature joining in a chorus of approval to the song of self-praise his own heart was singing, he almost danced along the road in his satisfaction and conceit.

"Smart piece of work that!" he remarked to himself, chuckling. "Poor old Ratty! My! won't he catch it when the Badger gets back! A worthy fellow, Ratty, but very little intelligence and no education. I must take him in hand someday, and see if I can make something of him."

Full of conceited thoughts such as these, he strode along, his head in the air, till he reached a little town ...

where the sign of "The Red Lion", swinging across the main street,

reminded him that he had not breakfasted that day.

He marched into the inn, ordered the best luncheon that could be provided, and sat down to eat it in the coffee-room.

He was about half-way through his meal when an only too familiar sound, approaching down the street, made him start trembling all over. The poop-poop! drew nearer, and the car could be heard to turn into the inn-yard and stop. Presently the party entered the coffee-room, talkative and gay, voluble on their experiences of the morning. Toad listened, all ears; at last he could stand it no longer. He slipped out of the room, paid his bill at the bar, and sauntered round to the inn-yard. "There cannot be any harm," he said to himself, "in my only just *looking* at it!"

The car stood in the middle of the yard, quite unattended. Toad walked slowly round it.

"I wonder," he said to himself presently, "I wonder if this sort of car *starts* easily?"

Next moment, hardly knowing how it came about, he found he had hold of the handle and was turning it. As the familiar sound broke forth, the old passion seized Toad and he found himself, somehow, seated in the driver's seat; as if in a dream, he pulled the lever and swung the car round the yard and out through the archway. He increased his pace, and as the car devoured the street and leapt forth on the high road through the open country, he was Toad once more, Toad at his best, Toad the terror, the traffic-queller, the Lord of the lone trail, before whom all must give way.

The miles were eaten up as he sped he knew not whither,

living his hour, reckless of what might come to him.

    "To my mind," observed the Chairman of the Bench of Magistrates, "the *only* difficulty in this case is, how we can make it sufficiently hot for the rogue and hardened ruffian we see cowering in the dock before us.

"He has been found guilty of stealing a valuable motor-car; of driving to the public danger; and of gross impertinence to the rural police. Mr Clerk, tell us, please, what is the stiffest penalty we can impose for each of these offences?"

The Clerk scratched his nose with his pen. "Twelve months for the theft, three years for the furious driving and fifteen years for the cheek — those figures tot up to nineteen years — so you had better make it a round twenty and be on the safe side," he concluded.

"Excellent!" said the Chairman. "Prisoner! It's going to be twenty years for you this time. And mind, if you appear before us again, upon any charge whatever, we shall have to deal with you very seriously!"

The Toad was dragged from the Court House to the grim old castle, whose ancient towers soared high overhead. There in the heart of the innermost keep, the rusty key creaked in the lock, the great door clanged behind him; and Toad was a helpless prisoner in the remotest, best-guarded dungeon in all the length and breadth of Merry England.